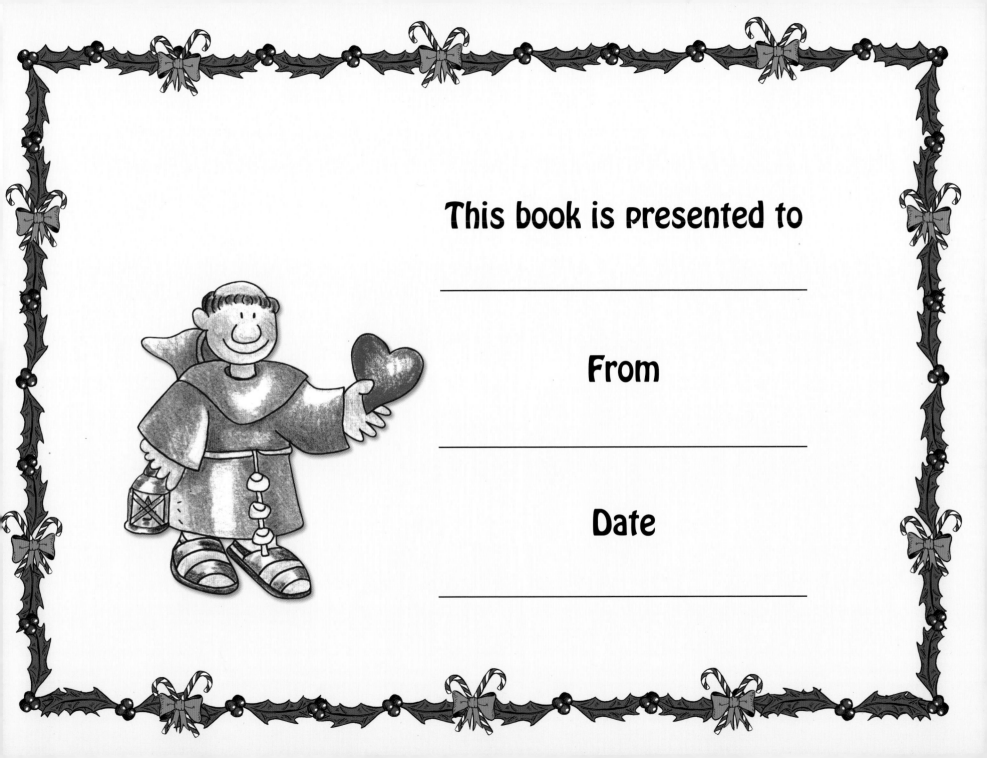

This book is presented to

_____

From

_____

Date

_____

Introduction

Christmas is a very special time. Leading up to that big event,
letters and e-mail requests are being directed to Santa Claus
who is keeping his little elves busy at the North Pole.

Most every little child is sleeping when those
sleigh bells ring as Rudolph, without air traffic control,
safely lands Santa's sleigh on rooftops of houses, apartments
and condominiums around the world.

Some get what they ask for and even more. Others don't.
After all, Santa is human and that's why, as hard as he tries,
he can't always get things right for others or even for himself.
This Christmas is one of those times.
Santa feels overwhelmed and calls Little Francis to the rescue.
As he helps Santa remember what Christmas is really about,
Santa's stress is relieved. May yours be, too!

Fr. Sereno Baiardi, OFM

From the Author

In a "me-me-me" centered world, material things often seem to matter the most,
especially during Christmas. For some, money isn't an issue when it
comes to buying gifts. For those who have no money, it becomes an issue.
Little Francis knew that the only way to help Santa was through prayer
that would take him back to that first Christmas.

God paid the ultimate price for our Christmas present—
the gift of salvation that money cannot buy. How can we ask for anything more?
What more important gift can we give than to share Jesus,
God's gift of love to the world?

A Blessed Christmas to you and to all.

Love,
Julie

Little Francis Helps Santa

written
by
Julie Hanna

illustrated
by
Lidia Mattiello Vallicella

published
by
Editrice Velar
&
The General Secretariat of the
Franciscan Missions, Inc.
P.O. Box 130, Waterford WI 53185

One Christmas time when Santa felt blue; his to-do list got harder to do.

The workshop was steaming.
The elves were all screaming.
Santa could hardly believe
it was almost Christmas eve.

Computer illiterate,
the elves did their best
checking e-mail
for every request.

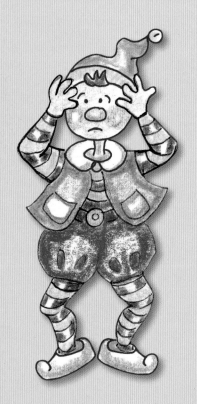

"Oh, no! Look, Santa,"
the surprised elves said.
"We didn't save the list;
we deleted it instead!"

Santa EXPLODED
and shook his beard.
The elves just muttered,
"Santa's acting weird."

They called Little Francis
who came right away.
When he saw the disaster,
he said, "We must pray."

They made a little circle
and joined their hands.
They started to remember
how Christmas began.

Renewed by the spirit
and no longer blue,
Santa apologized,
and the elves did, too.

Since the me-me-me had
gotten so out of hand,
Santa and the elves
designed a different plan.

They would write little notes,
put them in a sack,
then pile into the sled
with Santa in the back.

And with Santa,
who would appear?
Little Francis, Rudolph,
and the other reindeer.

Regardless of weather,
cloudy or clear,
Santa was happy that
Christmas was here.

With a jolly ho-ho-ho
Santa yelled,
"Is everybody ready?
It's time to go!"

At a low altitude,
the sled would go.
As the notes came down,
they looked like snow.

Some bounced off rooftops,
some landed on heads.
Turn the pages to see
what the little notes said.

There were
no reindeer.
Angels
appeared that
Holy Night...

It was the night
of Jesus' birth –
God's gift of love
to all on earth.

God has one list.
No one is excluded –
one gift for all,
you and I included.

The world is a circle.
Take someone's hand
and share the story,
why Christmas began.

The Author...

Julie is the author of **FRANCIS, LOVER OF NATURE, LITTLE FRANCIS LOVE NOTES** and **THIS HOLY NIGHT** (for which she received the Apostolic Blessing from Pope John Paul II). This fourth book, **IN THE BEGINNING... According to 'Little Francis'** is a turn-of-the century inspirational book that takes one back to the very beginning with God. Julie's depiction of St. Francis of Assisi through the simplistic creation of 'Little Francis' causes readers to fall in love with the 12th century saint. His devotion and love for the Creator was impeccable. Julie is the Communications Director of the General Secretariat of the Franciscan Missions, OFM, Inc. USA, an extension of the General Curia of the Friars Minor in Rome, Italy. She and her husband, The Rev. Stan Hanna, a pastor in the Evangelical Lutheran Church in America, reside in Milwaukee, Wis.

The Illustrator...

Lidia Mattiello Vallicella, Italian artist and teacher, specializes in painting, frescos, stained glass for churches, and sacred mosaics (you may find her artwork in Italy and overseas). She lives in Verona with her husband Giorgio and their two sons, Matteo and Enrico. For her technique, imagination, and sensibility, she has been recognized with awards and diplomas. Her bright illustrations based on simple texts are easy to comprehend and full of "spark" and joy. The General Secretariat of the Franciscan Missions invited her to follow in the footsteps of Sr. Chiara Amata as the illustrator and interpreter of St. Francis' adventures. Her drawings blend harmoniously with the words used by the author, Julie Hanna, a great friend of hers. They have worked together to create this small, happy book encouraging children and adults to find love, joy, and hope for the future. Lidia works in collaboration with her husband, Giorgio, an architect and dedicated volunteer for the past 30 years in designing and building schools, hospitals, churches and houses for the Franciscan Missions in Guinea-Bissau, West Africa.

The following items:
- •In The Beginning According to 'Little Francis'
- •This Holy Night
- •Little Francis Love Notes (in English, Spanish, and Italian translations)
- •Little Francis Buttons & Magnets
- •Little Francis Dolls
- •Little Francis Greeting Cards

are available at:

The Franciscan Missions, Inc.
P.O. Box 130
Waterford, WI 53185
ph: 262-534-5470 or fax: 262-534-5470
www. franciscanmissions.org

This book was published
with the cooperation of

Director
Fr. Sereno Baiardi, OFM

Text
Julie Hanna

Illustrations
Lidia Mattiello Vallicella

Graphic Design/Lay-out
Jeremy G. Hanna

Printed in 2009 by Editrice Velar, Gorle (BG) Italy